Lily's Big Animals

Story by Cameron Macintosh
Illustrations by Sumiti Collina

Contents

Chapter 1	From Pots to Panda	2
Chapter 2	A Big Problem	10
Chapter 3	An Exciting Idea	14
Chapter 4	A Garden of Big Animals	22

Chapter 1

From Pots to Panda

It was the weekend, and Lily's parents were doing some work around the house. They had put a lot of old things out with the rubbish.

Lily looked at the big pile of junk. "I'm going to use some of these things to finish my panda sculpture," she said to Mum and Peta.

Lily had been using pieces of junk to make sculptures of endangered animals.

Lily took two old pots from the rubbish pile.
"These pots are just the right size
to become my panda's ears!" she said.

"Your sculpture looks just like a real panda!" said Peta. "And it's the same *size* as a real panda, too!"

Using her tablet, Lily took a photo of her panda with the other creatures she had made – a gorilla, a snow leopard and a tiger.

That afternoon, with Mum's help, Lily uploaded the photo to her class web page.

"Hi, Mr Jones and Class 2D!" she wrote.
"I've made some sculptures of endangered animals,
so people can learn about them.
Let's find some other ways to help these animals!"

Chapter 2

A Big Problem

That night, Mum and Peta came into Lily's room.

"You are so clever, Lily," said Mum.
"I would never have thought to make animals with our old junk."

"Thanks, Mum," said Lily.

Mum went on, "Your sculptures are beautiful, but they can't stay in the front yard.
It's just too small for them."

"The backyard is too small as well," said Peta.

"Where can I put my sculptures, then?" Lily asked.

"We'll need to have a think about that," said Peta.

Lily couldn't settle down to sleep.
All she could think about were her sculptures,
and what might happen if she couldn't find
somewhere to put them.

Chapter 3

An Exciting Idea

The next day at school, Lily's friends told her how amazing they thought her sculptures were.

Lily couldn't tell them how worried she was about what her parents had said to her.

Lily needed some time to think. So, at lunchtime, she went for a walk around the school yard.

As she walked, she noticed a patch of long grass between the Year One classroom and the fence. She had an idea. This would be a good place for her sculptures. It could become a garden of endangered animals!

Lily went to see Mr Jones. She told him about her idea.

Mr Jones smiled. "That's a wonderful idea, Lily," he replied. "I saw the photo of your sculptures. They are great! The other children can make sculptures to go in the garden, too."

In class, Lily told everyone about the sculpture garden idea.

"That's exciting!" said her friend Jackson. "Maybe we can use the garden to fundraise for endangered animals."

"Yes!" replied Lily.

All through the week, Lily and her friends pulled out weeds from the new garden.

On Friday, Mum put Lily's sculptures in her truck and drove them to the school.
She helped the children place them in the garden.

Several other children brought sculptures
that they had made, too.
Soon, the garden was full of colourful sculptures
of endangered animals.

Chapter 4

A Garden of Big Animals

The next Friday, at lunchtime,
the whole school gathered at the edge of the garden.
Some parents were there, too.
As each person stepped into the garden,
Lily invited them to put some money in a box.

Ms Khalil, the principal, welcomed the crowd
and told them how proud she was of everyone's hard work.
"I also want to thank Lily from Class 2D," she said.
"This garden was Lily's idea."

When Ms Khalil had finished talking,
everyone walked around, looking at the sculptures.
Some people had their photos taken standing next to them!

Welcome to our Sculpture Garden!
HELP

Later, Lily counted the money in the box.

"Well done, everyone!" she said.
"We can give this money to a place
that takes care of endangered animals.
Our sculptures might even help
to feed some baby tigers!"